MW00877786

Printed in the United States of America

First Printing, 2018

Amazon Publishing Edition

www.amazon.com

Dedicated to our son, Logan.
May all your adventures be full of love and good friends.

armer Carol loved Honeysuckle Farm, her animal rescue farm. She had cows, pigs, geese, chickens, cats, dogs, horses, and the most magnificent herd of black sheep.

Early one morning, Farmer Carol headed out to
pick up a young sheep that
had been orphaned. His name was Hewey.
She thought he would make a beautiful
addition to Honeysuckle Farm.

Hewey was nervous to go to a new home.
He wished his friends could go with him to
Honeysuckle Farm, but he was ready for the new adventure.

"Honeysuckle sounds like a nice farm," Hewey thought.
"I bet they have green hills and a lot
of other sheep to play with."

Hewey then thought with excitement,
"I bet they even have the most delicious honey pies. Yum!"

Hewey loved honey pies more than anything.

Hewey watched anxiously as Farmer Carol's truck turned
down the dirt road leading to his home.
"She looks friendly," Hewey thought.
"I hope she likes me."
Carol parked and walked over to Hewey.
"Hello there, beautiful,"
Carol said as she smiled and reached out her hand to him.
Hewey let Carol pet him. She seemed gentle and caring.

Hewey decided he liked her.

Farmer Carol helped Hewey into her truck.
"You'll be comfortable in here," she said
as she covered him with a nice cozy blanket.

Hewey fell asleep as Farmer Carol drove them
to Honeysuckle Farm.

"Time to wake up, little sheep," Carol whispered to Hewey.
"We are home."
Hewey jumped up with excitement!
He couldn't wait to check out his new home.
Farmer Carol led him down the path toward the barn where
the other sheep lived.
Hewey loved seeing all the other animals that
were on the farm.
He couldn't wait to get to know them all.

Farmer Carol and Hewey arrived at the sheep barn.
"Here's your new home," Carol said with a smile.
"I hope you like it."

Carol opened the barn door, and
Hewey saw all the other sheep.
They were the most spectacular sheep he had ever seen.
They had shimmering black fur.

Hewey walked into the barn with Farmer Carol and smiled at
the other sheep.

"Hi, my name is Hewey," he said to the sheep.
"I'll let you all get acquainted," Farmer Carol said.
"You all be sweet to Hewey now."

She winked at Hewey and left.

Arthur, the Sheep of Police, stepped up and eyeballed Hewey.
"Well, aren't you a silly-looking sheep," he said.
"Where did you come from?"

"I was born on Snowball Farm," Hewey said.
"I lived there with my family until the owner sold the farm
and we all had to move away."

"Well, aren't you the chatterbox?" Arthur asked, and all the
other sheep laughed.

Hewey blushed and ran out of the barn.

Hewey ran up the hill and
sat underneath one of the large trees.
He began to cry.
He had always been good at making friends
and didn't understand why this time was different.

Hewey wished he could go back to Snowball Farm.

"Little sheep, why are you crying?" Ruby said.
Hewey looked up and saw an elegant light-brown horse
standing over him.
"The other sheep were mean to me." Hewey said.
"What did they say?" Ruby asked.
"They told me I was a silly-looking sheep,"
Hewey said with a sob.
"Oh, dear," said Ruby. "That won't do."

"Maybe I can help you," Ruby said.
"Sure," said Hewey, "How?"
"Well, I was once new to this farm too, you know."
Ruby smiled.
"I showed off some of my skills to help me fit in and make friends.
I can teach you those skills," she said.
"Wow. That would be great!" Hewey exclaimed.

"First, I will teach you to count," Ruby said.

Ruby spent the day teaching Hewey how to count to ten by stomping with his hoof.
At the end of the day, Hewey was ready to go.

"Thank you Ruby. I'm sure this will help!" Hewey said as he ran off to show the other sheep what he could do.

Hewey entered the barn and ran up to Arthur,
the Sheep of Police.
"Arthur, wait until you see what I can do,"
Hewey shouted with excitement
and began to count to ten with his left hoof.
"What are you doing?" Arthur laughed.
"Counting," said Hewey.
"Sheep don't count," said Arthur.
"You look absolutely ridiculous."
Again, the rest of the sheep began to laugh.

Hewey hung his head and went to sleep in his stall.

Hewey went to find Ruby first thing the next morning.
"Ruby," Hewey shouted,
"I've been looking for you everywhere.
Arthur says sheep don't count."
"Hmm. I'm sure I've heard something about
sheep and counting," Ruby said.
"I was positive that would help you fit in."

Ruby thought for a moment.

"I know. I can teach you to neigh," Ruby exclaimed.
"Everybody loves a good strong neigh."
Ruby showed Hewey how to do vocal scales and make a
lovely neigh sound.

"Okay, now go show the other sheep that magnificent neigh."
Ruby smiled with pride.

Hewey ran into the barn and stopped in the
middle of the herd.
He let out a loud and impressive neigh.
Immediately all the other sheep started laughing.
"Sheep don't neigh, you silly boy. Neighing is for horses.
Real sheep baaaa." Arthur chuckled.

Again, Hewey hung his head in disappointment and went to
sleep in his stall.

Hewey left the barn early in the morning
and sat under his favorite tree on the hill.
Ruby came galloping up and said with shock,
"I can see by your face that the neighing didn't work!
I'm so surprised. Those are some tough sheep."
Hewey shook his head, and Ruby plopped down next to him.

They sat in silence for a little while.

"I've got it!" Ruby shouted. "I'll teach you to jump."
"Don't bother," said Hewey. "They will never accept me."
"Don't give up, little sheep," Ruby said.
"Let me teach you this one last skill.
I'm certain it will work!"
"Okay," Hewey said reluctantly.

Hewey really enjoyed learning to jump.
He was laughing and smiling all day.
He was grateful to have a friend like Ruby the Horse
who cared enough to teach him new skills.

**By the end of the day, Hewey could
leap over fences as high as Ruby!
"Ruby, thank you for teaching me to jump today,"
Hewey said as he laid down under the tree.
"My pleasure." said Ruby as she laid down next to him.**

"Whew. It's been a long day," Hewey said.
"I certainly am tired!"
"Me too, little sheep," Ruby said. "Let's get some sleep,
and we can show the herd what an amazing jumper you are
tomorrow. I'll go with you this time."
Ruby yawned and began to close her eyes.
"It's such a lovely night," Hewey sighed.

He was finally beginning to feel at home
on Honeysuckle Farm.

Hewey and Ruby were awakened by a loud screeching noise.
"What is that?" Hewey asked.
"I think it is the fire alarm," Ruby yelled.
"Hurry, it looks like the barn is on fire!"

Ruby and Hewey ran as fast as they could to the barn.
The back of the barn was on fire, and all the sheep were
trapped inside their stalls.

"Help us!" they shouted with panic.
"Don't worry," Hewey said.
"Ruby and I will get you out!"
Hewey looked at Ruby and cried,
"Hurry, Ruby. We don't have much time."
Ruby moved quickly and began to open the stalls on the
right side of the barn.
Hewey leaped into action and used his new jumping skills
to reach the latches on the left side of the barn.

"Run and wake up Farmer Carol,"
Hewey shouted at the sheep
as he and Ruby rescued the rest of the herd.
Once everyone was safely outside, Ruby and Hewey ran out
of the barn and collapsed.
They were covered in ash and dirt.
Arthur, the Sheep of Police, approached Hewey.
"Where did you learn to jump like that?" he asked.

"Ruby taught me," Hewey said quietly.

"I have never seen a sheep jump that high before."
Arthur said sternly. Then he began to smile kindly at Hewey.
"We are certainly lucky that you aren't like all the other
sheep, aren't we? Welcome to the family, Hewey."
Arthur nodded and walked away.
The rest of the herd ran up to Hewey,
shouting in excitement.
"Thank you, Hewey! Can you teach us to jump like you?"

They surrounded Hewey, and he smiled a big toothy grin!
Ruby swelled with pride at the sight.

Once the excitement died down, Hewey ran over to Ruby.
"Did you see them?" he asked.
"I sure did." Ruby giggled.
They both laughed, and Hewey said,
"Thank you for being my best friend, Ruby."
They walked together to sit under the tree on the hill.

The End

Made in the USA
San Bernardino, CA
13 December 2018